You're All My Favorites

Sam McBratney

illustrated by Anita Jeram

CANDLEWICK PRESS
CAMBRIDGE, MASSACHUSETTS

O
nce upon a time

there was a mother bear,

a father bear,

and three baby bears.

A first baby bear.   A second baby bear.

And a third baby bear.

Whoever tucked them in at night

always said the same thing to them:

"You are the most wonderful baby bears

in the whole wide world!"

One night, after Mommy Bear

had tucked them in, and after she had said,

"You are the most wonderful baby bears

in the whole wide world,"

the baby bears began to wonder.

"But how do you know?" they asked
their mommy bear. "How do you know
we are the most wonderful baby bears
in the whole wide world?"

"Because your daddy told me,"

said Mommy Bear.

"When your daddy saw you on the night

you were born, he said—

and I remember it very well—he said,

'Those are the nicest baby bears

I have ever seen.

They are the nicest baby bears

anyone has ever seen!'"

That was a good answer.
The three baby bears snuggled
down as content as could be.

But one day, the first baby bear began to think. He wondered if the other two bears were nicer than he was. They had patches, after all, and he did not. Maybe his mommy really really liked patches.

And the second baby bear began to wonder.

Maybe Daddy loves the other two

more than me, she thought.

They were boy bears, after all,

and she was not.

And the third baby bear

began to worry.

I'm only the littlest, he thought.

Everybody's bigger than me!

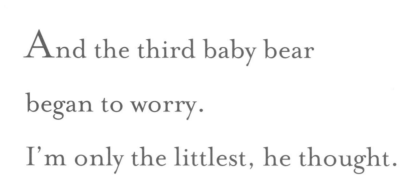

So that night the three baby bears asked their daddy bear,

"Which one of us do you like most?

Who is your favorite?

We can't all be the best."

"Yes, you can," said Daddy Bear. "I know you can because I heard your mommy say so. When she saw you" — and Daddy Bear picked up the first baby bear to give him a cuddle— "she said, 'That is the most perfect first baby bear that anyone has ever seen.'"

"Even with no patches?"

"Patches don't matter at all," replied his daddy, as he tucked him in.

"And when your mommy saw you" —Daddy Bear picked up the second baby bear— "she said, 'That is the most perfect second baby bear that anyone has ever seen.'"

"Even if I'm not a boy?"

"Girl or boy, it makes no difference," said her daddy, and he hugged her tight.

"And when your mommy saw you" — Daddy Bear

lifted the last baby bear into his arms—

"she said, 'That is the most perfect third

baby bear that anyone has ever seen.'"

"Even if I'm the littlest?"

"Biggly or littley,

we love you just the same.

So there. Three favorites.

You're all my favorites!"

And the best baby bears in the whole wide world

went to sleep as happily as could be, because

that was a good answer, too.

For all *my* favorites:
Sam and Daniel and Jack
and Adam and Ella ~ *S. M^cB.*

For Joe, Danny, and Kitty ~ *A. J.*

Text copyright © 2004 by Sam McBratney
Illustrations copyright © 2004 by Anita Jeram

First edition in this form 2007

This edition published specially for Kohl's © 2007 by Candlewick Press, Inc.

Library of Congress Cataloging-in-Publication Data is available.
Library of Congress Catalog Card Number 2004045169

ISBN 978-0-7636-2442-2 (Trade edition)
ISBN 978-0-7636-3492-6 (Kohl's edition)

2 4 6 8 10 9 7 5 3 1

Printed in China

This book was typeset in Mrs. Eaves Roman.
The illustrations were done in watercolor and pencil.

Candlewick Press
2067 Massachusetts Avenue
Cambridge, Massachusetts 02140

visit us at www.candlewick.com